Bound by Blood: Lies, Loyalty, Legacy

The Reluctant Mafia Princess Series

Sydney Brown

A PenPossibilities Collaboration with
Elecca Maxwell

Bound by Blood: Lies, Loyalty, Legacy

THE RELUCTANT MAFIA PRINCESS SERIES

Sydney Brown

A PenPossibilities Collaboration with Elecca Maxwell

Published by TLM Publishing House

Alpharetta GA.
https://www.ttpublishinghouse.com
Copyright © 2023 TLM Publishing House

Bound by Blood: Lies Loyalty Legacy – Prequel

ACKNOWLEDGMENT

This new series is an exciting stretch outside my comfort zone.

The mafia world is raw and gritty, so developing this series to include some historical accuracy and realistic stories is the big goal. We were up for the challenge!

I want to thank someone for their contributions with research, storyline creation, and editing. As part of our new collaboration program, PenPossibilities, we create a short read book together, and I walk my collaborator through the writing and self-publishing process.

Elecca Maxwell, a new best-selling author, and graduate of the I'm the Writer-Publishing Professional certification program, has been a great writing partner in this book project. Thanks, Elecca!

CONTENTS

THE PERFECT LIFE

'Buzz... buzz...buzz...' 'Buzz... buzz... buzz...'

'Arrrgh!' I pull my arm out from under my cozy covers and fumble to reach the snooze button. 'Just a few more minutes of rest.' I groggily mumble as if justifying my procrastination.

'Buzz.. buzz.. buzz..' 'Buzz Buzz Buzz.'

'Grrrrrrrrhh!' "What's wrong with you? Freakin alarm." I grumble and hit the snooze button with more force than necessary.

'BUZZ BUZZ BUZZ BUZZ BUZZ'

I swing my legs out of bed and rub my bleary eyes, trying to shake off the sleep. Feeling a familiar ache in my head, I rub my temples, trying to ease the pain. It's been happening more lately, and I'm not sure what's causing it.

'BUZZ BUZZ BUZZ BUZZ BUZZ'

"Okay, okay, I'm up," I say aloud, reaching for the alarm clock and hitting the off button, this time with more force— the buzzing stops.

Taking in a deep breath while I look at the clock, *it's early*, much earlier than I'm used to waking up, but today is a big day for me. It's my first college interview.

I can't believe I'm a senior in high school. Determined to get into my dream college and study business, I worked hard to maintain good grades and participate in extracurricular activities.

"Good morning, Cassie!" Mom calls out from the kitchen.

"Morning, Mom," I reply as I head to the bathroom to get ready.

I take a deep breath as I get dressed and do my makeup. I don't want to go into the interview looking like I feel.

My dad pops his head into the bathroom. "Big day today, Casabella. How are you feeling?"

"A little nervous but mostly excited," I answer, trying to hide my discomfort.

He smiles, his eyes lighting up with pride, "That's the spirit! You're going to do great!" His soothing voice and the quirky way he calls me Casabella reminds me how lucky I am. I don't know why he calls me Casabella. I was born Cassandra, but I realized early on that Cassie drew a lot less attention from the bullies at school. But for my dad, I'm always Casabella.

"Thanks, Dad. You always know just what to say." Almost choking on my words.

"I will see you downstairs. Mom is making breakfast for your big day." Dad whoops with excitement.

As an only child, I've always been the center of my parents' attention. My parents? Oh, they're quite a unique duo.

My mom, she's like a total control freak and perfectionist but in a good way. I don't know what happened in her youth, but she's determined to make sure I'm safe and ready for anything that comes my way.

I'm talking self-defense classes, martial arts, the whole deal. She's taught me always to be alert, trust my gut, and never let my guard down.

But my dad, he's all about enjoying the moments, you know? He's the one who's taught me all about poise, elegance, and being classy while living my best life. I swear, he must be a closet Brad Mondo fan! He's like my personal etiquette coach, always reminding me to mind my manners but keep my curiosity alive.

They've given me this crazy mix of skills and values that have shaped me into the person I am today. Even though my dad may look like the tough one, he's just a giant teddy bear. I'm definitely a Daddy's Girl. I know Mom has my best interest at heart, but I'd love to see how these two got together.

They're more like Jekyll and Hyde than Bonnie and Clyde, but somehow, they make it work. I've never heard a cross word from either of them in the past seventeen years!

I look in the mirror one last time, grab my bag, and make my way downstairs for breakfast. Halfway down the stairs, I am met with the aroma of Mom's homemade blueberry waffles.

"Mom, you made my favorite!" I squeal with excitement, "Thanks, Mom. You always know how to make me feel special. How did I get so lucky to have the best parents?"

Mom gives me a gentle hug and says, "I didn't give you the gift of life; life gave me the gift of you." her eyes sparkling with pride.

"Now sit down and eat breakfast to prepare for your interview." Mom directs me to the plate of waffles she places on the table where I sit.

##

"Good luck, honey!" my mom says, hugging me as I approach the door.

"You got this, kiddo," my dad adds, giving me a pat on the back.

Another freaking awesome day in Lake Grove, my chill little suburban spot just outside Chicago. It may not be the wildest, most happenin' place on Earth, but it's got its own vibe.

The streets are lined with these great little trees and the neighbors? They're like the friendliest people ever, always waving and saying hi to each other. It's the kind of place where everyone knows everyone.

Heading to school, I can feel those damn jitters creepin' in. What if I screw up during the interview? What if I don't make the cut?

5

Damn it, Cassie! I gotta stop lettin' these doubts mess with my head! *Okay, just remember all the hard work you've put in. You've got this,* I think...

As I step onto the school grounds, there's Sarah, my ride-or-die since we were kids. She's always had my back, no matter what.

"Hey, Cassie! How are you feelin' about the interview?" Sarah greets me, all pumped and supportive.

I take a deep breath, trying to calm my racing thoughts. "I'm a bit nervous. It's a huge opportunity."

Sarah playfully bumps my shoulder. "Girl, you got this! All that hustlin' and grindin' is gonna pay off. Just go in there and show 'em who's the boss."

Her words give me a shot of confidence, like an adrenaline rush. "Thanks, Sarah. Your belief in me means a lot."

She winks, a glint in her eyes. "Hey, I've seen you in action. Damn, girl! You've got charisma for days. They won't know what hit 'em."

##

Throughout the day, I find myself feeling more and more confident. I feel like I nailed my interview. I even had a chance to tour the campus, and it's the perfect fit for me.

As I head home from school, I know my parents are eagerly waiting to hear about my day.

"I'm so proud of you, Cassie. You're going to go far," my mom says, hugging me.

"Me too, Boss," my dad adds, giving me a pat on the back. I always giggle when Dad calls me boss. I swear, sometimes the man lives in an old 40s mafia movie.

Over dinner, we discuss my future plans, and I mention how I hope to follow in their footsteps and become a successful business owner someday.

"I have a feeling you'll be even more successful than we ever were," my dad says with a wink.

As we finish dinner, my mom hands me a letter. "This came for you today, honey. It looks like it's from the college."

"That's odd," I say. "I just had the interview today," peering intently at the envelope.

I open the letter, my hands trembling.

"*Congratulations, you have been accepted to...*" I trail off in a look of disbelief.

"How could this be?" I look to my parents for some sort of reassurance. I don't think this is how it works.

"That's fantastic, Cassie!" my mom exclaims. "We knew you'd get in."

But as I read further, I can feel my heart racing.

"It looks like an anonymous donor has already paid my tuition in full."

"What?" my dad says, looking at me in surprise.

"That's weird," my mom agrees.

I try to brush it off, not wanting to spoil the moment. "I'm just happy to have been accepted," I say with a smile.

I head upstairs to my room and lay on my bed staring at the ceiling, still confused about how I received the acceptance letter the same day as the interview.

To add to the confusion, my parents didn't seem to bat an eye. Is this normal? I'm not one to look

8

a gift horse in the mouth, but this sure doesn't seem normal.

As I lay in bed, my mind wanders to the mysterious donor. Who could it be, and why did they pay for my tuition?

A feeling of unease settles in my stomach, and I can't help but wonder if there's more to this than meets the eye, and why aren't my parents freaking out about this too?

Bound by Blood: Lies Loyalty Legacy – Prequel

THE CREW

Senior year is flying by, and I'm killing it on all fronts. I snagged the top spot as the debate team captain, I'm running the business club like a boss as the president, and I even started my own jewelry business on the side.

It's awesome having a business of my own before I even graduate. I started making rings from silverware, and it's taking off like wildfire.

Thursday after school, Sarah and I link up with Tyler and Sophia at our favorite coffee joint. Tyler isn't like the other boys from school. We've known each other since we were kids, growing up as neighbors.

We may never have even met if not for sharing a front yard. The universe seems to have my back, though, with putting the best besties in my path.

I met Sophia during a martial arts class one summer, and we instantly clicked. Her parents are a little creepy. We joke that they're in a secret

11

club for swingers or something. They have a weird vibe, but at least they seem good to Sophia.

The coffee house is buzzing with people, and the smell of brewed coffee hits our noses.

"Guys, can you even comprehend that we're almost done with senior year?" Tyler blurts out, sinking into the cozy corner booth.

"No way! It feels like we just started, and now graduation's around the corner," I respond, sliding in next to him.

Sophia shoots me this admiring look, eyes sparkling. "Cassie, how the heck do you manage all this and still slay? Spill the tea, girl!"

Her words hit me, a mix of pride and a hint of self-doubt. Gotta keep it cool, though.

"Well, you know, it's all about finding that balance," I say, trying to sound chill. "Time management and staying organized are the keys."

Sophia raises an eyebrow, not buying it for a second.

"Oh, come on, don't hold back, Cass," she insists, overflowing with curiosity. "There's gotta be some secret sauce to your success. Share the deets!"

I chuckle, feeling a bit bashful under their intense questioning.

"All right, all right," damn... I give in, grinning. "I guess I've mastered the art of multitasking. I've got my color-coded planner and sticky notes plastered everywhere, and I know when to take a breather and recharge. Oh, and a little caffeine boost never hurts."

Sarah playfully raises an eyebrow. "Ah, the secret's out! Coffee, huh?"

Sophia bursts into laughter. "No wonder you're always bouncing with energy! Coffee is your superpower."

I nod, laughing along. "You got it! It's my secret weapon for taking on the world."

Tyler throws up his hand, "Ladies and gentlemen, I present to you Cassie, the Boss! Together, we're an unstoppable dream team, ready to conquer everything."

Laughter fills the air, lifting our spirits. These friends of mine know exactly how to bring out the best in me.

As we keep chatting and catching up on life, I feel this overwhelming sense of gratitude for their unwavering support. They've been there for me through thick and thin, and I know I wouldn't have made it this far without them.

As my mind goes into one of my mental movies, I imagine each of us going our own ways when we graduate. I try to picture how we all get what we want in life and still stay together as the dream team, and I know we'll probably end up like everyone else before us, going in different directions and reliving our good old days at reunions.

"Not us. I refuse to let that happen," I interrupt whatever conversation the others were having as I drifted off.

"What's that, Cassie?" Tyler asks, "You off in your head again? Who's after us this time?" He laughs but waits for an answer.

"Oh geez, I'm sorry. I guess I was. I just am afraid we're going to lose track of each other as we start this whole adulting thing. I don't want to lose you guys," I blink away the would-be tear.

"No way, girl," Sarah, ever the cheerleader, grabs my hand, causing a chain reaction until we're all locked into one circle, "This dream team is forever. If I had a knife, we'd sign a blood oath.

I'm that sure that we'll always be together!" We erupt into laughter, a few tears, and sighs.

Tyler pulls out one of his blood sugar lancets and presents it to us, his expression obvious, "If you want, we can make that blood oath right here and now. I'm just sayin'."

"You're crazy, Tyler. How would we even do it? Why would we do it? And what is the penalty for breaking the oath? If we're going to do something extreme, we need to spell out the rules," As I lay out my protests, I realize I've talked myself and the others into doing it.

"Rule one," Sarah grabs a pen from her purse and writes on a clean napkin, "No matter what adult life hands us, we four will forever have each others' backs when called on for help." We all nod in agreement.

"Rule two," Tyler grabs the pen and napkin, "No matter what, we four will see each other at least four times a year, even if it means video calls."

"That's doable," I say as I grab the napkin, "Rule three. No matter what, we four will never put anyone in our lives who don't understand our friendship," I smile as love overflows.

"Your turn, Sophia," I point the napkin toward her and see that she's not as excited about this blood oath as the rest of us.

"You okay, Soph?" I ask.

"Yeah," she stammers, "It's just, will this hurt? How much blood are we talking about here? Is this witchcraft? Or are we just like blood brothers or something? Do we need to cut ourselves to prove our commitment to each other? Why do we need to prove it? Why are we calling them rules? I mean, this is like a marriage proposal and immediate wedding."

"Holy shit, Soph," Sarah interrupts, "Calm down. You don't have to prove anything. I think it's a fun idea. If you don't want to come up with a rule or participate, you don't have to. But now we know who our weakest link is!" Sarah cackles as she playfully shoves Sophia.

For just a moment, we all sit in awkward silence, sipping our coffees or looking around.

"Oh, Rule four!" Sophia screeches with excitement, "No matter what, we four swear never to lie to each other. If asked directly, not even a white lie is allowed." Sophia nodded proudly.

"Whoa, that just escalated," Tyler laughs. "We go from not wanting rules at all to not even letting surprise birthday parties in our futures?"

"Nah, white lies and surprise birthday parties are allowed. So, as long as we don't ask directly, we'll be good. We just can't lie when questioned about something. It'll be like the ultimate game of truth or dare!" Sophia giggles as she finishes writing her rule.

"Okay, I'm game," Tyler nods, "What's the penalty for breaking the oath? Death? Excommunication? A stink bomb in the mail?"

"I say we don't have a penalty," I break in, "We don't really have to do this. I didn't mean to start us going down this crazy rabbit hole," I look at each face to accept their disappointment.

"No way! We're doing this," Sarah commands as she grabs the lancet from the table, pricks her ring finger, and squeezes blood onto a saucer, "One, two, three. Three drops of blood, taken from my ring finger, to forever pledge my allegiance to our dream team crew!"

Tyler grabs the lancet and pokes into his ring finger, "Okay, now we're pledging allegiance?" he squeezes onto the top of the three existing drops on the saucer, "One, two, three. I guess I'm in!"

I look at Sophia, wondering if this is a situation where I go first or if I let her go first. I never learned the proper order of blood oaths in any of the etiquette classes my parents sent me to.

"My turn," Sophia offers, giving me another moment to grasp what we're doing here. She grabs another napkin and tries to wipe off the germs or blood from the lancet and then softly laughs at herself, realizing we're somehow going to put our combined blood back into us, so wiping off germs is irrelevant at this point.

"I pledge allegiance to 'we four' and commit to follow our four rules. One, two, three."

I grab the lancet and follow suit, "Okay, guys, we now are sitting here, literally bleeding into a saucer in a public coffee house. I love you guys more than life itself, but we need to wrap this up. We're gonna get the wrong kind of attention here." I counted three drops, and we all look at each other.

"I take it none of us have thought this any further? What do we do? There's not enough to drink it, and all we did was poke our fingers, so we can't put it back into us unless we poke ourselves again." I speak the obvious.

"It only takes like twenty-six seconds for something on our skin to absorb into our bodies. I read that somewhere. We can stir it up, and just each put a dot of it on our ring fingers where we pricked ourselves, maybe? Even if it doesn't go back in the same hole, maybe some will sink in?" Sophia offers.

"Sounds good to me," I stir the blood with a clean fork and dab a dot onto my ring finger, "I pledge my allegiance to 'we four' for as long as we should live."

Each person follows, and as we complete this crazy backwoods blood oath, Tyler asks, "Do we need to chant or anything? Mine's already dried. Are we bound now?"

We all laugh as Sarah says, "I guess it's a good thing that none of us know how to do a real blood oath. I'd be more worried if we did. I love you guys, though, for real. Even without the blood, I swear allegiance, too.

Sophia pours a little bit of her coffee over the remnants of blood on the saucer, "Let's just get rid of the evidence and make sure no one else sneaks in our little oath without invitation," she smiles.

"Girl, you were a little too comfortable getting rid of the evidence. I know who I need to call when I have to hide a body one day!" I laugh, causing everyone to laugh until we exhaust ourselves.

"I love you guys. I feel better. Thanks. Maybe it's all your blood in me or just knowing you'll have my back, but thank you."

I look across the table again and feel the full magnitude of not just a best friend but realizing I have everything I'll ever need in life right at this table.

##

Senior year flies by. My crew and I remind each other of our blood oath at least daily. It's become a running joke. I don't know if it's the oath or realization that we're running out of time together, but someone always seems to be walking in the front door like they all changed their addresses to my place.

My parents' standing invitation, "The door is always open to any friends," is being taken literally. But today, it's all about me and Calculus. No interruptions if I hope to make valedictorian.

>>*Beep beep*

Startled by the text on my phone, *Wait a minute! I don't recognize this number!*

>>*"Congratulations on your acceptance, Cassie. I hope you enjoy your time at college."*

What the hell? Who could be texting me from an unknown number? And how did they know about my college acceptance already?

I ignore the text, hoping it's just a random well-wisher who I don't know. But over the next few days, more texts start coming in. They're all from the same unknown number, and they all seem to know things about me that no one else should know.

>>*"Your parents must be so proud of you, Cassie."*

>>*"I can't wait to see what you do with your future."*

>>*"Remember, Cassie. There are people who believe in you and want to see you succeed."*

The texts are starting to feel more and more ominous. Who is this person, and what do they want from me?

I can't take it anymore. I text back.

<<*"Who are you? How do you know about my college acceptance and my parents?"*

The response comes back quickly.

>>*"I'm just someone who wants to see you succeed, Cassie. Someone who believes in your potential."*

I try to press for more information, but the person doesn't reveal anything else. I'm left feeling even more uneasy than before.

As the days go by, the texts continue to come in. Sometimes they're encouraging, and other times they feel almost threatening.

>>*"Remember, Cassie, your success is our success."*

>>*"We're watching you, Cassie. Make us proud."*

I feel like I'm being watched, like someone is always lurking in the shadows, waiting for me to slip up.

At nighttime, lying in bed, I hear a noise outside my window. My heart starts racing as I try to stay quiet and listen. But I don't hear anything else, and eventually, I drift off to sleep.

By morning, I decide to tell my parents about the texts.

##

I approach my mom, anxiety tightening its grip on my chest. With a deep breath, I gather my courage and decide it's time to confront her.

"Mom," I say, my voice quivering. "Can I talk to you about something?"

She looks up from her laptop, her brows furrowing with concern. "Of course, sweetheart. What's on your mind?"

I hesitate for a moment, unsure of how to approach the subject. Finally, I blurt out, "I've been getting these weird texts lately. They're from an unknown number, and the messages are just...weird."

Her expression changes, her eyes widening with alarm. I can sense her tension and her uneasiness, but I need answers.

23

"Dad, too," I continue, my voice trembling. "Are you guys aware of this? Do you know who could be sending them?" I hand my phone over to my dad. He scans through the messages, and his gaze stops. He hands the phone to my mother, and she begins to read the messages.

There's a heavy silence in the room, and for a moment, I fear I've said or done something terribly wrong. My mom's face tightens, her jaw clenches, and her eyes flicker with a mix of anger and fear.

"Stop responding," she snaps, her voice laced with an intensity I've never heard before. "Do you hear me? Just stop!"

Her sudden outburst takes me aback. This isn't the calm and composed mother I've always known.

"Oh, trust me, I'm so creeped out. I blocked the number already. Do you know who it is?"

Before I can utter another word, my mom and dad storm out of the room, their hurried footsteps echoing down the hallway. The door slams shut behind them, leaving me alone with a whirlwind of confusion and a sense of danger hanging in the air.

It's evident that there's more to this story, something my parents are trying to shield me from. Their overreaction and hasty departure only amplify my concerns. Are they trying to protect me? Is there a real danger lurking behind those messages?

As I sit there, my mind racing with possibilities, I feel a mix of frustration and fear. I need to know the truth to understand what's happening. But for now, all I can do is wait and hope that my parents will eventually share their secret for my own safety and peace of mind.

##

So, one day I'm just like, "You know what? Screw it. I'm gonna do some serious digging." I march myself down to the financial aid office, determined to get some intel on the mysterious donor. I mean, come on, spill the tea, right? But, man, those folks are tight-lipped. They give me the whole spiel about how the donor wants to keep their identity hush-hush. Can you believe it? Seriously?

I raise an eyebrow, not buying their explanation. "Come on. You gotta give me something. Who's this secretive benefactor?"

The financial aid officer shrugs, a sly smile playing on his lips. "Sorry, kiddo. It's all on a need-to-know basis, and you don't need to know."

I lean in closer, determined not to be shut down so easily. "But don't you think it's a little bizarre? I mean, this mysterious donor, hiding in the shadows, funding our education. It's like we're characters in some secret society."

The officer chuckles, glancing around as if checking for eavesdroppers. "I hear you, but some donors prefer to stay anonymous. It adds an air of intrigue, you know?"

I cross my arms, not willing to back down just yet. "Well, they've certainly nailed the mysterious part. But it'd be nice to at least know who's behind this incredible opportunity."

The officer's eyes twinkle. "I get it, kid. Curiosity gets the best of us sometimes. But trust me, whoever it is, they've got their reasons. Just enjoy the benefits and focus on making the most of this opportunity."

I let out a sigh of frustration, realizing that this mystery might remain unsolved. "Fine, I'll play along. But mark my words. One day I'll uncover the truth. And when I do, it'll be a story for the ages."

The officer chuckles, patting me on the shoulder. "I admire your determination, kid. Just remember, sometimes the unknown can hold its own kind of magic."

Not one to give up, I decide to take my investigation to the college's alumni association. Maybe they'll have some insider knowledge or, dare I hope, some juicy deets to share. With determination in my stride, I enter their office, ready to crack this mystery wide open.

"Hey there," I greet the alumni association representative with a smile. "I've got a burning question for you. Who's the secret donor behind all this financial aid?"

The representative raises an eyebrow, their expression guarded. "Sorry, but that information is strictly confidential. We're not at liberty to disclose the identity of our generous donors."

I lean forward, my curiosity piqued. "Come on, spill the beans. What's the big secret? Are they some kind of undercover billionaire or what?"

The representative chuckles, shaking their head. "I'm afraid I can't reveal anything, not even a hint. It's all about respecting the donor's wishes for anonymity."

Frustration gnaws at me, but I refuse to back down. "But what's with all the secrecy? It feels like we're dealing with some classified government operation here."

The representative leans back in their chair, a knowing smile playing on their lips. "Well, let's just say that sometimes the allure of anonymity adds a certain mystique to the act of giving. It allows donors to focus on the impact they're making rather than seeking recognition."

I cross my arms, still determined to uncover the truth. "I get that, but it's just so intriguing. I mean, imagine having that kind of power to change lives and remain unknown. It's like being a superhero without a cape."

The representative nods, their eyes gleaming with understanding. "It can be quite remarkable, indeed. But remember, it's generosity and the opportunities that matter the most. Focus on what this aid means for you and the doors it can open."

I let out a sigh of resignation, realizing that this mystery might be harder to crack than I anticipated.

"All right. You win. Thanks for your time," I walk out and head home, accepting that I need to get the answers from somewhere else because clearly, finding the truth is not happening today!

##

After what feels like an eternity, the tension in the house begins to subside. Days pass, and my parents' initial overreaction fades into a more composed demeanor. It becomes clear that they are taking the situation seriously and are determined to protect me.

One evening, after dinner, my mom and dad exchange a knowing glance. It's a silent signal that they have made a decision.

"Cassie," my mom says gently, "We're sorry for reacting like we did. We just want to protect you."

My dad nods in agreement, his eyes filled with a mixture of love and worry. "We've been worried sick about those texts, sweetheart. It's not safe to engage with someone you don't know. Stranger danger and all that," my dad smiles, "We love you, Cassie, and your safety is our top priority. That's why we've decided to take some measures to protect you."

Curiosity tinged with apprehension fills me. I wonder what they have in store and what steps they've taken to ensure my well-being.

My mom reaches into her bag and pulls out a sleek, brand-new phone. She hands it to me, her hand trembling. "We got you a new phone, Cassie, with a new number. It's an extra precaution to cut off any connection to whoever is sending those messages."

I take the phone from her, feeling a mix of gratitude and relief.

"We've already transferred your contacts and important information to the new device," my dad adds, his voice soothing. "We want you to feel safe and reassured, Cassie."

"Thank you," I whisper, my voice choking with emotions. "I appreciate it."

My dad places a comforting hand on my shoulder. "We'll do everything we can to keep you safe, Cassie. If anything else happens, remember that you can always come to us."

##

A couple of months go by. I'm just chillin' in my room, mindlessly scrolling through my phone. Then, bam! I stumble upon this news article that grabs my attention. It's all about this entrepreneur who made a fortune with his ad agency. And they're an alumnus of my college and a big-time donor to the scholarship fund.

My heart starts racing as I read on. Could it be? Is this the anonymous donor who covered my tuition?

For the next few days, I go full-on detective mode, diggin' deep to uncover more about this mysterious entrepreneur. I devour every article, watch every video. And then, bam again! I come across a name that sends shivers down my spine.

The entrepreneur's name is John Reynolds, CEO of one of the biggest marketing agencies in the country. I recognize that name in an instant. John

Reynolds is one of my heroes, someone I've admired for ages.

But hold up, it's not all sunshine and rainbows. As I keep reading, I discover that John has a shady past. He's been accused of all sorts of sketchy stuff over the years, like embezzlement and fraud. The allegations haven't been proven, but there's enough evidence to make you go, "Hmm, something's fishy here."

Suddenly, it all starts clicking. The pieces of the puzzle fall into place. John Reynolds must've paid for my tuition as his way of making up for past mistakes. Maybe he sees a bit of himself in me, a young and ambitious hustler.

But as much as I appreciate the gesture, I'm torn. Should I accept money from someone with such a controversial past? And what does it mean for my future? As I lay in bed that night, I realize I've got a whole lotta thinkin' to do.

\#\#

The next day at school, as I chill with my crew at our usual hang-out spot, Brew-bakers, we're all taking a moment to soak it in. Graduation's just around the corner, and it's hitting us hard.

Sophia breaks the silence. "Hey, can you believe it? We're about to dip from this place and dive headfirst into the unknown. It's exciting and kinda scary, you know what I'm sayin'?"

Sarah, doodling on her notebook, nods. "Totally, girl! It's like we're standing on the edge of a cliff, ready to free fall into a whole new chapter of our lives. No clue what's waiting for us down there."

Tyler kicks back; his voice filled with anticipation. "But that's the dope part, man. We get to reinvent ourselves, find out what we're really passionate about, and carve our own path. It's a fresh start, and we gotta make it count."

Sophia stares into space, deep in thought. "I'm gonna miss this place, though, you know? The halls we've walked a billion times, the classrooms where we've laughed and struggled. But at the same time, I can't wait to explore new places and meet new peeps and stuff."

Sarah's eyes light up, her voice all fired up. "And we've got each other. We four, always. We've been through thick and thin, and no matter where life takes us, we'll always have that bond."

As the convo gets real, the energy cranks up. We start talking about dreams, goals, and what we want to achieve. There's an electricity in the air 'cause we're all itching to get out there and hustle for our passions.

I raise my voice with determination. "We ain't lettin' fear hold us back. This is our moment to shine, to grab hold of the present and squeeze every ounce of joy and knowledge outta it. We owe it to ourselves to make this count."

Tyler nods, grinning wide. "Hell yeah, Cassie! We're young, we're hungry, and we're ready to take on whatever life throws our way. We ain't wastin' a second of this opportunity. We're grabbin' it by the balls."

As our voices blend together, a sense of purpose washes over me. Yeah, change is scary, but we're in it together, ready to take on whatever comes our way.

GRADUATION DAY

Ugh, I jolt awake on graduation morning to the most annoying sound ever blaring from my stupid alarm. My eyelids feel like bricks, and I struggle to gather my foggy thoughts. Like, seriously, today's the big day, and it's like my brain can't even process it.

I stumble out of bed, feeling like a zombie, and somehow manage to make my way downstairs. The smell of breakfast hits me like a punch in the face in the best possible way.

My parents are in full-on chef mode, bustling around the kitchen, creating a feast fit for royalty. It's become a thing now for my friends to gather at my house because my parents are total rock stars when it comes to cooking up these Italian meals for special occasions.

I walk into the dining area, and my eyes nearly pop out of my head. The table is decked out with these awesome balloons in all sorts of vibrant colors, and there's this banner hanging up that screams, "Congratulations, Graduates!" It's like a

35

party explosion. All I can do is grin from ear to ear, taking in the sheer awesomeness of it all.

I head into the kitchen, and there's my mom standing there with this beaming smile. "Good morning, Miss Graduate!" she exclaims. Her excitement is contagious. "Can you believe it's here?" she asks, her voice filled with a mix of pride and disbelief. It's like she's just as amazed as I am that this day has arrived.

I grin back at her with excitement. "I know, Mom. It's like I'm living in a dream or something. But hey, I'm ready to dive headfirst into this day, no matter how wild and unpredictable it gets. Bring on the craziness!"

Dad plops down a tower of pancakes on the table; his eyes shimmer with pride. "You've worked hard for this, Casabella. We're so proud of you."

Just as we're settling in, the front door bursts open, and Sarah storms in, her infectious grin lighting up the room. "Cassie, it's finally here! Graduation day, baby! Can you believe it?"

I give her a tight squeeze, "Heck yeah, Sarah! We've been waiting for this moment for years. I can see us now, strutting our stuff across that stage, tossing those caps high in the air like we own the world."

Tyler saunters in a few moments later, rocking a boyish grin and tousled hair like he just rolled out of bed. "Yo, Cassie, Sarah! Ready to ditch these halls and conquer the world?"

I chuckle and playfully punch him on the arm. "You bet, Tyler! It's our time to shine."

Sophia follows behind, confidence and sophistication oozing, her smile radiant. "Morning, fam! Can you feel that energy? Today's gonna be one for the books!"

We dive into our pancakes, and the trip down memory lane begins. Waves of nostalgia hit, and we share our favorite high school shenanigans.

Sarah leans in, mischief sparkling in her eyes. "Remember that time we snuck into the school after hours and got busted by the security guard?"

Tyler raises an eyebrow. "How could I forget? We thought we were stealthy ninjas until we tripped over our own shoelaces."

Laughter fills the room, carefree and contagious.

"What about when we convinced our chemistry teacher we needed to conduct a 'scientific experiment' in the courtyard? Dude's face was pure gold!" Tyler revels.

I nod, transported back to those unforgettable days.

Sophia nudges me, grinning. "Hey, y'all remember that spontaneous road trip last summer? The bonfire party on the sand was legendary! We danced under the stars and made memories that'll stick with us forever."

As the morning rolls on, the excitement in the house reaches an uproar. We finish breakfast, trading playful jabs and reliving our high school escapades.

Tyler glances at his watch and jumps up from his seat. "All right, peeps, it's time to gear up! Graduation's calling our names!"

Sarah nods, with nervous excitement in her eyes. "You're right, Tyler. We gotta grab our stuff and make our way to the school."

I glance at these three, that I've affectionately called my crew for years now. Their faces reflect a whirlwind of emotions— "We've been through it all, you know?" I soften and try to hold it together.

Sarah grabs my hand, giving it a reassuring squeeze. "Cassie, no matter what happens next, we've got each other's backs. Remember? Ride or die, bitches!" Sarah catches a disapproving glance from my mom, who then breaks into a smile as well.

I grin, overflowing with appreciation. "For real, Sarah. We're tight like family, and I'm beyond lucky to have you all in my life. Now, let's climb into that limo and do this up in style!"

##

"Yo, check it out," I say, pointing towards the school as we pull up. "The place is packed, dude!"

Sarah chimes in, intense excitement in her voice. "I can feel it, guys. The vibes and the energy are strong."

We step out of the limo and pause, taking a moment to absorb the scene before us. The outdoor stage is decked out with gorgeous flowers, standing against the backdrop of a clear sky. I am literally tingling with excitement.

Sarah lets out a breathless sigh. "Wow, just look at that stage! It's like a dream, guys. We're really here!"

Sophia nods, a twinkle of pride in her eyes. "I can't believe it. All those late nights, hard work, and sacrifices led us to this moment."

Hand in hand, we strut through the stanchions, following the path to our future, ready to own the final act of our high school journey.

Tyler stops, makes a runway pose, and declares, "All right, gang, let's burn this mutha down!"

Sophia adds, her voice filled with conviction, "Hellz, Yeah! Together. We four."

As we step onto the main field area, our jaws practically hit the floor. The entire field is transformed into this epic graduation spectacle—rows upon rows of chairs, the stage decked out in banners, and a massive crowd of hyped-up faces already milling about.

Tyler lets out a low whistle, his eyes wide with awe. "Holy crap, guys! Look at this setup! It's like a freaking stadium!"

"No kidding! Sarah injects, "This is beyond anything I imagined. It's like we're about to rock a concert!"

Sophia can't contain her grin, her eyes scanning the scene. "I can't believe this is all for us. It's like a dream come true!"

We stand there for a moment, taking in the breathtaking sight before us.

"Hey, check it out," I point out, nodding toward a handful of police officers. "I guess they're here to make sure everything goes smoothly."

"Looks like we have to nix the plan to strip down and run across the stage naked," Tyler laughs, causing the rest of us to let out a belly groan.

As we maneuver through the crowd, my eyes are drawn to these huge banners that create makeshift walls. They're like a snapshot collection of our senior year. "Dude, check these out," I say, "These banners are epic!"

Sophia adds, her voice heavy with nostalgia, "It's like a time machine, dude!"

I nod in agreement, a warmth spreading through my chest. "They're a reminder that we have the power to create change, no matter how small our actions may seem. Together, we can move mountains."

Tyler pats me on the back, a proud grin on his face. "Damn right, Cass. By the way, don't forget to tell your parents thanks for delivering us in style. I know it's gonna be the first question out of my mother's mouth, right after *'Did they actually give you a diploma?'*"

"Oh, please. Your mother knows you'll get your diploma. As for the limo, no worries. We'd talked about having a limo for all the big milestones since I was little. I think they were more disappointed than I was when Paul and I broke up right before prom. They think of you all as their kids too. To be honest, I've been a little jealous at times," I admit as I spot an event photographer.

"Hey, guys, look!" I whisper, "Let's get some pics."

Sarah's eyes light up, "YES! We need to seize the moment."

We're like, super conscious of our poses, making sure we're in the perfect spot for the photographer to catch our mega-watt smiles. We huddle up, our arms linked, forming this awesome tight-knit crew, all set to capture this moment forever.

Tyler raises an eyebrow. "All right, everyone, let's show off our best 'we're conquering the world' smiles!"

Laughter ripples through our group as we strike a pose, trying our best to balance between looking confident and not bursting into giggles.

"Just be natural, guys," Sophia advises, her eyes twinkling with mischief. "We want these photos to truly reflect who we are."

The photographer motions for us to strike different poses, urging us to let our personalities shine through.

Sarah, always the adventurous one, raises her arms up high, a symbol of triumph. Her laughter bursts through the air. With her head thrown back and a carefree expression on her face, the camera clicks, capturing that vibrant spirit, freezing it in time for eternity.

"Come on, let's get in tight!" the photographer directs. "Show that unbreakable bond!"

We all gather closer, our smiles merging into one collective beam of joy. As our hands shoot up, forming the familiar "rock on" sign.

"We Four!" I shout the words echoing our unity.

Click. The photographer snaps the picture.

As we download the app for the event photos, we hear some sort of commotion in the distance.

"Hey, guys! Something's going on back there," Sarah whispers, her eyes widening with curiosity.

Tyler grins mischievously. "Oh, you know I love a good drama. Let's check it out! I wonder whose mom showed up drunk to graduation."

Sophia rolls her eyes. "OMG, do you remember last year when Craig's mom did that? In a class this size, I guess it's impossible to avoid some sort of drama. But let's not get too carried away. We still have the ceremony to attend."

As we approach the back of the stands, we hear a group of people spreading the gossip like wildfire.

"Did you see that woman causing a scene? She's adamant about getting inside!" I hear someone whisper.

"I heard her say her daughter is one of the graduates. They won't let her through, though," another person adds.

Intrigued, we begin to cautiously inch closer, trying to catch more snippets of the conversation.

I speak up, with concern in my voice, "Hey, excuse me, what's happening with that woman? Why won't they let her in?"

One of them turns to me, almost whispering. "Apparently, she showed up late and doesn't have the proper credentials. Security is being strict about it, but it seems like she's really desperate to see her daughter graduate."

"Oh man, that sucks. I'd hate it if my mom didn't get to see me graduate," I say.

"As if! Your parents were probably the first ones in the building, Cass," Sarah teased, causing us all to laugh.

"You're not wrong," I agree.

An officer speaks up above the crowd, "Graduates, you need to clear the area."

We make our way to our assigned seats. I begin to sense the weight of the moment still lingering in the air. I can't bear the silence, and curiosity tugs at me. "I wonder who that woman is trying to see. Did you guys catch a glimpse of her daughter?"

Sarah shrugs, her brow furrows with intrigue. "I couldn't see from where I was. But it makes you wonder, right?"

##

As we settle into our spots, I feel the anticipation ramping up. The view of the stage is set for the climax of our high school adventure. I can hear the swish of robes, the hushed chatter, and the occasional bursts of laughter filling the air.

Tyler leans over, his voice buzzing with nervous energy. "Dudes, I can't lie; I'm feeling a bit jittery. Like butterflies on steroids, you know?"

Sophia grips his hand with a reassuring smile on her face. "Just take a deep breath and soak it all in, bro."

I try to turn and scan the crowd of faces, on the lookout for my folks. "Man, I hope Mom and Dad show up in time for my speech. This is a major moment, and I want them to be here."

Sarah pats my shoulder, "Don't sweat it, Cassie. Your parents wouldn't miss your valedictorian speech for anything. They're out there in the sea of faces. Seriously, don't worry about it. They won't let you down. They'd kill to see your speech! I wish mine could stand even to sit next to each other. Yours are probably holding hands and telling each other how great they are. You've got the perfect everything. You're like a freakin' princess."

I hear my name being called over the speaker system. It's my turn to step up to the podium. I feel my heart pounding in my chest as I make my way to the stage as if it could burst at any second. I take a deep breath, adjusting the mic to my level. The crowd hushes, all eyes locked on me.

I steal a glance at my crew, their supportive smiles fueling my confidence. Sarah throws me a thumbs-up. I shoot her a reassuring grin. I think I see my parents about half the way back.

The good news is we have big screens on the stage so everyone can see as we get our diplomas, but that also means they can all see every hair out of place or if I start to ugly cry.

Standing tall at the podium, about to unleash my speech, I sense the crackles and excitement buzzing from the crowd.

"Good morning. Friends, family, and classmates..."

What the hell, man? I smile awkwardly as I see this strange woman in a pair of jeggings and a black leotard running down the center aisle. She looks too old to be a student pulling a prank, but she's got quite a sprint going.

Is that... Wait a minute... is that the same woman that was causing a scene behind the stands? I can't tell if she's running toward me? Or away from something else?

Of course, it'd happen when I'm on stage... can't have just a regular moment to rock my speech. Hopefully, someone will catch her and make her sit down.

I feel my mind going in a dozen directions at the same time. Do I go ahead with my speech? Where are all the adults? Someone needs to say something... Do something. I've never seen this lady before, but I hold my breath and hope that she makes it to her goal.

I pause at the podium, smiling uncomfortably, waiting for someone to do something. I feel the smile fall from my face as I realize that she's 100%

not running as a prank. Her eyes are locked on... me?

I dunno what the hell is going on, but this lady is crazy-running. She's gonna trip and face plant if she doesn't slo—

Bang Bang.

THE AFTERMATH

Oh my fucking-Gawd! Was that...?

I duck at the sound of the shots. Living outside of Chicago, we know what bullets sound like, and that was definitely bullets.

Oh, Gawd.... My eyes scan forward to try to make sure the woman running is okay. I can't find her. Everyone is running all over.

I stand here, frozen, scouring the crowd to try to figure out if somehow this is a gag. Hoping against hope. But it isn't.

I see the blonde woman's body on the aisle; her body sprawled in a way that I immediately know, she's dead.

"Oh god." I stand there frozen, staring at her lifeless body as the entire field falls into chaos. People begin screaming and running in every direction. The noise is deafening.

"Cassie!"

I hear my name and snap back to the reality of the moment. I think I hear more shots fired and realize that I've failed my mother's number one rule always to evaluate your environment and know where your exits are.

"Cassie! Get down!" I hear my dad yelling, but I don't see him.

Thud! Just like in the TV shows, Someone clips my feet, and I'm on the ground with someone lying on top of me.

"Get off of me!" I scream as I try to punch and kick my way out from under whoever has attacked me. He weighs too much, though. I can't even squirm. I'm trapped.

"Cassie. Hold still." My dad whispers to me as he shifts his weight to let me catch my breath. "I don't know what's going on, but just hold still. When I count to three, I need you to get to your feet and run as fast in the direction I point you. Nod if you understand what I'm saying."

I nod. I don't know where he's going to point me or even how he's going to point me, but I know my dad is going to protect me. I take a deep breath and wait.

"One. Two. Three. RUN Cassie! Just keep running."

"I love you, Daddy. Are you coming with me?" I cry out as I start running toward the side of the stage where I was pointed. There are still people running in every direction, and I hear sirens nearby.

I reach out my hand and look for my dad, but he's gone. I'm alone, and I don't know who's shooting. I do what I'm told, and I just run until I'm outside the staging area.

Out of nowhere, an officer grabs me, "This way. You're safe. I'm the police. Keep going toward the bus to your right. Hurry. Hurry."

"My parents are in there. I think someone was shooting."

"We know, miss. Just go get on the bus for now."

I'm pushed toward an old school bus where the police are loading us all to be evacuated. I collapse into a seat and as the bus fills, the sounds of the cries get louder and louder. I can't understand what anyone is saying. I close my eyes and just pray that my mom or dad will find me soon.

##

My hands tremble as I hold onto my phone. The girl sitting next to me, with tears streaming down her face, looks just as terrified as I am.

She sniffles and wipes her nose with the back of her hand. "I can't believe this is happening. What the hell is going on? How many people got shot?"

I glance at her, my voice shaking. "I have no idea. It was chaos back there. Shots, people running... I've never seen anything like it."

She nods, her eyes filled with fear. "Do you think it's over? Are we safe now?"

I shake my head, unable to offer any reassurance. "I don't know. I hope so. But until we get more information, we need to stay alert."

The bus starts moving, and the noise of conversation fills the air. Some students cry. Others try to call their loved ones. I try to call my dad and then my mom, but my calls won't go through. I set up a group text to them both, "I love you guys. Please reply asap. I'm on a bus. I don't know where they're taking us."

I try to focus on my breathing to calm the racing thoughts in my mind. I hear voices behind me. "I can't believe this shit, man. Graduation is supposed to be a celebration, not a fucking nightmare."

The guy replies, his voice cracking. "I know, right? It's like everything changed in an instant. I just want to see my family and make sure they're okay."

I can feel a lump forming in my throat as I hear their words. The same desperation, the same longing for safety and reassurance. We're all in this together, clinging to hope amidst the chaos.

A police officer walks through the aisle, trying to calm the students. "We're taking you to a safe location. Just hang in there. We're doing everything we can to ensure your safety."

Turning to the girl next to me, "Do you think they caught the shooter?" I ask, my voice barely above a whisper.

She shrugs, her eyes filled with concern. "I don't know. It happened so fast, and there was so much panic. I just hope they're able to bring an end to this madness soon."

We sit in silence for a while; the sounds of muffled sobs and whispered conversations fill the air. The bus ride feels long, each passing minute an agonizing reminder of the unknown.

The bus finally comes to a stop, and we're escorted into a large community center that has been set up as a temporary shelter. Red Cross volunteers and emergency personnel are on hand, providing comfort and support to the shaken students. We all walk through the interior doors, and I realize we could be walking straight into a slaughter, unwittingly to our death. Did we really confirm that the escorts were real police officers? My mind begins to run rampant, and I look up for the first time to see what is ahead of me.

I hear my name being called. "Casabella," I turn around to see my dad. My heart skips a beat as I rush into his arms, feeling the warmth and strength of his embrace.

"Dad," I say, my voice choking with emotion. "I was so scared. I thought I'd lost you."

He holds me tighter, reassurance in his voice. "I'm here, Cassie.

As we cling to each other, I scan the room, desperately searching for any sign of my mom. But she's nowhere to be found. The weight of uncertainty settles heavily upon my shoulders, and my heart aches with worry.

"Dad, where's Mom?" I ask, my voice trembling. "Why isn't she here with you?"

My dad's expression softens, his eyes reflecting the pain that I feel. "We don't know, honey," he replies, his voice filled with sorrow, "We're doing everything we can to find her. When I heard the shots, I immediately ran toward the stage to get to you, and I just... left her there." Dad's voice cracks, his shoulders fall, and his eyes make it clear that he is concerned.

Tears well up in my eyes, and I struggle to hold them back. "But she has to be okay, Dad. We can't lose her. How many people got shot? Was it just that lady running down the aisle?"

"Cassie. Calm down. We'll get answers soon. I just know that your mom is going to be fine. Let's see if there's a meeting spot. I was just lucky to have found you.

##

In the midst of the chaos and uncertainty, I spot familiar faces in the crowd. Tyler, Sophia, and

Sarah made it to the community center too. Relief floods through me as we reunite, embracing each other.

Tyler's eyes are filled with a mix of worry and relief. "Cassie, I'm so glad you're safe," he says as he pulls me into a half hug, half kiss, his voice filled with concern, "I was terrified when we couldn't find you. We thought the bullets were going right at you."

Sophia nods in agreement as she runs to throw her arms around me, tears streaming down her face. "We were all so scared," she says, her voice trembling.

We huddle together, grasping onto each other, trying to wrap our heads around the madness unfolding around us.

"Cassie, I'm going to keep looking for your mom. Keep your phone turned on, and don't leave this spot! I will stay within eyeshot," Dad commands as he rushes toward a group where someone is talking from a megaphone.

I nod and hold onto Sarah's hand. "Have you guys found your parents yet?" I ask.

"Yeah, luckily, they were all sitting near each other, so we all got onto the same bus," Sophia

58

nods, hugging everyone, "We came looking for you since it looked like the crazy woman was running toward the stage. We wanted to make sure you weren't hurt."

"Why would I be hurt? She wasn't coming after me, was she?" I ask.

"Man, it sure looked like she was on a beeline toward you, but someone took her out. Did you see her fall? She like flew ten feet or so before she landed. I don't know much about guns, but that couldn't have been caused by a handgun," Tyler answered.

Whispers and murmurs ripple through the crowd, carrying bits and pieces of information. And then, I catch a snippet of conversation that sends shivers down my spine.

"Did you hear what she said? The woman who got shot... she mentioned her daughter was up there on the stage."

Those words hang in the air, adding another layer of mystery to this whole nightmare. Who is this woman? What the hell was she doing heading towards the stage? And who is her daughter?

I try to close my eyes and recall who was on the stage with me, but I just can't see anything in my mind other than her eyes focused forward, evidently running for her life.

I thought she was running toward us, but now it seems she was running away from someone trying to hurt her. Questions continue to flood my mind, but answers seem miles away.

Tyler notices the TV hanging on the wall, playing a news story about my dad's heroic actions. He exclaims, "Hey, turn that up!"

The news anchor's voice fills the room, recounting the terrifying events of graduation. I glance to my dad, who's standing near a window, his eyes glued to the screen.

"They're calling him a hero," the news anchor announces. *"His quick thinking undoubtedly saved lives. As the details of today's attack are unraveled, we'll keep you in the know. At this time, we recommend that everyone stay in your homes and keep your doors locked. No one has reported seeing a shooter as of yet."*

I watch as a complex range of emotions cross my dad's face. Pride shines through for doing what he believed was right in the face of danger. But there's also worry etched on his features, concern for my mom's well-being. He sees that I've spotted him and comes over to where we are sitting on the floor.

As we sit there, the TV continues to play in the background, and the news stories seem to be on continual replay, making us relive those moments every quarter-hour.

Tyler leans against the wall, frustration dripping from his voice. "The cops better catch the sicko who did this. We need answers."

Dad nods somberly. "They're doing everything they can, but it's going to be tough without any leads."

As the hours drag on, my worry intensifies. Many reunited families are documented and allowed to leave. *Where is my mom? Why hasn't she shown up yet?* The knot in my stomach tightens with each passing minute.

Suddenly, a commotion erupts near the entrance of the community center. Heads turn, and there she is, my mom, making her way through the crowd. I run towards her, a mix of relief and confusion flooding my senses.

"Mom!" I call out, my voice shivering with a blend of emotions. "Where have you been? We've been so worried!"

61

She gives me a weak smile. Her voice filled with a hint of frustration. "Oh, sweetheart, I'm so sorry. The bus I was on had a flat tire, and we were stranded for hours. It was a complete mess. But I'm here now, and I'm safe."

"But why didn't you call? We were all so scared. We didn't know if you were safe or not."

"I lost my phone. It was just one thing after another, Cassie. I'm here now, and that's what matters."

"Hey, pumpkin, let's just get everyone home for now," my dad interrupts, "We can drop the kids off on the way. Maybe order a pizza and decompress. It's been a helluva day."

"You can say that again!" I fall under his right arm as he gently puts his left arm around Mom's waist and leads us all to the waiting limo. "Wow, Dad, you save my life and keep tabs on the limo for us, too? I'd call you Superman if we didn't live in the wrong Metropolis!"

##

The next morning... I wake up with a knot of fear and uncertainty in my chest. The shooting has rocked our community, and it seems like the police investigation is going nowhere. Frustration and anxiety hang in the air as the police search for any shred of information.

By noon, the world seems to have forgotten what happened, and the news has gone from 'Stay home and lock your doors.' to 'It's a beautiful day for a picnic.' I get that not everyone felt the same fear that we did, but how does the world move on so quickly? There's barely even a one-page story on my news app.

I did get an email from the school that we'll all be getting our diplomas in the mail. Clearly, my speech wasn't that big of a deal, all things considered, but they could have at least mentioned me or something.

God, I'm such an attention whore. I can't believe I'm worried about people seeing me give my speech when at least one person was killed yesterday.

I'm meeting up with the crew at the Brew-bakers tonight. I think I'll take a nap and try to chillax with a hot bath. Get my mind off of everything.

I mean, I could have gone live on our school page with my speech, though.

63

Argh. *Stop being such a shallow bitch and close your eyes*, I scold myself.

##

That evening, at the coffee shop, huddled around a table, Sarah glances around the room and asks, "Any updates on the investigation? Have you heard anything new?"

I let out a sigh; my frustration is evident. "I caught a snippet of what my parents were saying last night. They mentioned there are no witnesses, no evidence. It's like it was just the one woman shot, and the shooter vanished into thin air. I would have sworn I heard more shots, but I honestly don't remember most of the night already."

Sophia nods. "Has anyone heard anything about the woman who was shot? How can nobody know who she is? It's all so mysterious."

I take a sip of my coffee, but it does little to calm my troubled mind. "It's scary, you know? Not knowing who's behind all this. Every time I step outside, I feel like someone's watching."

Sarah chimes in, understanding my sentiment. "I get it, Cassie. I've heard people talking about beefing up security with cameras and stuff."

"I can't wrap my head around this happening in our town," Sophia whispers, her voice trembling. "It's like we're trapped in a nightmare, but here we are, sipping coffee, and the world moves on."

"I just wish we had answers. I mean, was it a one-time thing, or is there a serial killer out there? Are we safe?" I ask, voicing the question that hangs heavy in the air.

"I wish I knew," Sarah responds, "but for now, I think we all need to stay on guard and get our butts home before dark, just in case."

THE CARDS

I walk into the house, hearing Dad's voice drifting from the kitchen. "Hey, Casabella, looks like you received some more cards," he calls out, his tone filled with curiosity and a hint of excitement.

I reply with a grin, "Alrighty then! Let's see who loves me the most!"

Dad chuckles as I make my way to the kitchen. He's sipping on his coffee, the smell of freshly brewed java filling the air. The stack of envelopes sits beside him, waiting to be opened.

I give Dad a hug and grab the envelopes from the counter. "Thanks, Dad! Why so many? We don't even have this many relatives! Oh well, I'm not complaining. Time to see what surprises await me."

With a skip in my step, I head up to my room, clutching the stack of cards like precious treasures. The anticipation builds with each step. I know it's not supposed to be about the money or gifts, but if I'm telling the truth, I can't wait to soak in all the love and support... and, of course, see who sent money.

Entering my room, I flop onto my bed and spread the cards out. They come in all shapes and sizes, each one holding a piece of someone's heart. I pick up the first card, opening it to reveal a heartfelt message from my favorite aunt.

Her words bring a smile to my face and a check for $20. "Thanks, Aunt Karen," I whisper.

"Money pile," I announce to myself as I create the process for who gets a thank you call, card, or email. "Five to forty-nine gets a card. Over fifty gets a thank you call, and no gift gets a canned thank you email."

I make sure to write the amount of each gift on the card it came with, so I don't get myself confused. "Maybe everyone should get the same treatment no matter what they send. I mean, it's the thought that counts, right?" I wonder aloud. But so many of these people, I barely know. Mom and Dad gave me the list of who to send invitations to from their business associates, so calling them would be Awk-ward.

"Solid process," I affirm.

I continue opening the cards, savoring the handwritten messages and words of encouragement. As I reach the bottom of the stack, I notice a mysterious envelope. Its plain appearance stands out among the colorful cards. There's no name, no sender's address.

"Whoa, wait a minute! This thing feels heavier than the others." I tear it open, and my eyes nearly pop out of their sockets.

"No way!" Inside the plain envelope are several one-hundred dollar bills, staring at me like a pot of gold. But hold on; there's no message, no explanation. "What the hell? Who sent this?"

I count each bill, one at a time. The sound of the bills crinkling between my fingers is exhilarating. "One... two... three..." I mutter under my breath, my heart racing.

"Four... five... six..." I place each bill neatly on the bed, my fingers tracing the edges of the crisp currency. The stack grows before me, each bill representing a small fortune.

I wonder who would send me such a substantial amount of money without any explanation. My mind races through possibilities, trying to piece together the puzzle. Was it a mistake? A generous gesture from a secret benefactor?

"Seven... eight... nine..." I count, the weight of the money in my hands making the reality sink in. This is no ordinary occurrence. It's a moment of unexpected fortune that certainly has my attention.

Finally, I reach the last bill, holding it up triumphantly. "Ten! A thousand bucks!"

My racing mind tries to connect the dots. And then it hits me like a lightning bolt. "Ah ha!" It's gotta be Dad! He's always been the sneaky type, slipping me some extra cash now and then, always telling me to keep it hush-hush from Mom. That rascal!

A big grin spreads across my face. Dad's done it again, pulling off another one of his secret surprises. He knows how to make me feel special, adding that touch of mystery. What a legend!

I gently tuck the money back into the envelope and write *Dad's Secret 1K* on the card in tiny letters so random sets of eyes won't know. I find a hiding spot for it in my drawer, making sure it's safe.

"I love you, Daddy!" I yell down the hall, assuming he's waiting for some sort of reaction.

"Love you too, Boss. How much did everyone love you?" he asks.

"Everyone seems to think I'm about Eight hundred and forty-five dollars special, and of course, my special card," I let him know I know his secret.

"That's quite a haul. Maybe you'll double it when you graduate college!" he yells to me and chuckles.

COUNTDOWN

As I sit and think about having to pack my belongings in cardboard boxes, it hits me. I'm moving out in just under a month. Leaving behind the familiar walls that hold a lifetime of memories is both exciting and bittersweet. The time has come for me to spread my wings and show the world what I'm made of.

Today, the goal is to Marie Kondo the crap out of my room. Everything that doesn't bring me joy is going to the donate pile. I grab a marker and write "Donate" on the side of one box.

The next box will be saved stuff. I write CVE Storage on that one, and then I write DORM on the next box. Dad said we'd buy new dorm stuff once we get there and see what we have to work with as far as space, so my goal is to only take a couple of boxes along with my suitcases of clothes, and the rest will go to the storage barn out back.

It's surprisingly easy to fill six boxes of clothes and knick-knacks into donation boxes. I'm struck by how little the things around me every day have meant to me. *Eh, maybe it means I value people and not things. That's a good thing*, I tell myself.

I'm down to the final two drawers in my dresser. My parents joke about how we have too many junk drawers around the house, and I realize these are my own version of junk drawers. Anytime I know I want to save something but don't have a special place for it, it gets thrown in one of these drawers.

The first one, I pull out of the dresser and dump it out onto the bed. There are hundreds of little odds and ends here. Overwhelm starts to set in, so instead of dealing with it, I grab the final drawer and dump it out onto my bed too.

Misery loves company, I think to myself.

This drawer is where all my love notes since grade school, report cards, and all my old school photos are. Ah, the blue ribbon from field day in the standing broad jump back in third grade. How random of a thing to hold onto for so long.

I plop down onto my bed and start spreading everything around, digging, turning piles of papers over, looking for treasures.

"Hey, Cassie, need any help?" Sarah calls out from the doorway of my room.

Looking up, a smile tugging at the corners of my lips. "Sure, Sarah. Just going through all the treasures of my life."

"Oh, fun. Let me at it," Sarah rushes to my side and scooches me over, "OMG, girl, who's Brad Palmer? First love?" She opens the letter from him and reads silently. "Oh, a summer love. You were only thirteen that summer. How have I never heard of him before? What else have you been holding out on me?" she teases.

"Look at this picture of me in kindergarten... or was that first grade? Gawd, my mom dressed me in a full formal gown for the holiday concert. What was she thinking? I don't even remember this, but I'm on the stage alone. I guess I've been groomed to be on stages all my life," we both laugh.

Then I remember the last stage I was on, and all the memories of seeing that poor woman shot down in front of me flood my mind. *Shake it off, Cassie*, I tell myself.

"Oh, look, cards!" Sarah grabs the stack and starts tearing into them and separating the cards from the envelopes.

"Wait!" I command, "I haven't even done all the thank you cards for the graduation cards yet. I don't want to lose the names of who sent what. I think I got everyone's names on the cards with what they sent, but I need to keep them with the addresses. My mom had me send a ton of invitations to people I don't even know. I thought it was dumb at first, but hey, it ended up with almost a thousand dollars in gift money!"

"Ah, sorry. Got a little excited," Sarah starts matching the cards back with the correct envelopes, "Sorry, girl, this one doesn't have an address on the envelope at all. How do you know which one this goes with?" Sarah holds up the card my dad sent me.

"Oh, that's from Dad. He didn't sign it," I grab the card and show her both sides to prove it's nameless. "He gave me a thousand dollars. I assume he didn't want Mom to know. He's not said a single word about it. Not even a wink when I hinted at a thank you. I'm sure Mom would lose it if she knew he gave me that much money on top of all the other things they've had to pay for the past few months."

76

"Your dad may have given you a different card then. This one has a message on the back," Sarah reads, *My dearest Victoria, with deep love and admiration. V. "* Sarah looks up at me, puzzled.

I grab the card, "No, this was the one. It had ten, one-hundred-dollar bills in it. What the hell?" I shuffle through the items on the bed to triple-check that this is the same card. "It's addressed to me on the envelope; look," I point to my name to prove to myself, as much as Sarah, that the thousand bucks was meant for me.

Sarah's face wrinkles in confusion. "So, maybe they wrote onto the wrong card? Maybe you should ask your parents if any of their business associates have asked about the money. They may have put it into the wrong envelope or something," Sarah suggests.

"I guess I should," my mind reeling with curiosity. "I wonder who Victoria is and why did this card end up in my hands? I think I'll try to ask Dad when he's alone, in case it's from him after all, but it sure is starting to look like that was meant for someone else," I sigh heavily, "Well, crap."

"What if," Sarah grins, "We try to figure out who Victoria is, and maybe she'll be so rich, she won't even care that she missed out on the money card!"

"Yeah, maybe. I've gotta get through these last two drawers, though. Today isn't the day I start failing to meet or exceed my goals. Do you want to go grab the guys and come back and grab me and hang out tonight?" I ask, hoping she'll agree without questions.

It's times like this that I realize I might be a bit too focused or short-sighted, but when I get an idea, I'll obsess about it until I've exhausted every possibility I can come up with. Right now, I have a thought, and as much as I love her, Sarah is only going to distract me.

As if reading my mind, Sarah smiles, "Sure. Sounds good. I'll text when we're almost here. I'll go see what other drawers I can get into today! This is fun!" she giggles as she walks toward the front door. "Bye, Mrs. E," she yells out as she walks past my mom in the living room.

Like a maniac on a mission, I rush to my laptop and start searching all the Victorias on social media. My friends. My parent's friends. Anyone's mutual friends.

For an Italian family, I shouldn't be surprised that there are several of them. But none seem like they have recently celebrated anything that would earn them a thousand bucks.

"Nope. It was definitely meant for me," I decide as I close the laptop. A moment of guilt rekindles my quest, though, so I grab my thank you cards and head out to the living room to hang out with my mom.

I'm not sure how I'm gonna do it, but 'Operation Find Victoria' is now officially launched.

COLLEGE

Standing in my packed-up room, surrounded by moving boxes and memories, Sarah shows up to see me off to college, her gaze filled with a mix of excitement and sadness.

"You're really leaving, Cassie," she says softly, her voice tinged with a hint of melancholy.

I nod, a bittersweet smile playing on my lips. "Yeah, it's time to start this new chapter of my life. College, independence, and all that jazz."

Sarah sighs and looks around, her eyes lingering on the walls adorned with photographs capturing moments of our laughter and friendship. "It feels strange, you know? Like everything's changing so quickly. We've been through so much together, and now you're off to conquer the world."

I reach out and clasp her hand, offering reassurance. "Change is a part of life, Sarah. We've always supported each other, and that won't change. Distance won't phase us. Ride or die, remember?"

She nods, her grip tightening. "You're right. I just can't help but worry. What if something goes wrong? What if you find yourself in a place where you feel lost and alone?"

I take a deep breath, understanding her concerns all too well. "I won't lie, Sarah. The graduation incident shook me to my core. It made me question everything, including my decision to pursue college. But I can't let fear dictate my choices. I need to face my fears head-on and trust that I have the strength and resilience to overcome any obstacles that come my way."

Sarah's eyes glisten with tears, and she pulls me into a tight embrace. "You're stronger than you know, Cassie. Don't ever forget that. And if you ever need someone to lean on or a familiar voice to guide you, I'm just a call away."

Her words warm my heart, reminding me of the unwavering support I have with her. "Thank you, Sarah. Your friendship means the world to me. We may be physically apart, but our bond will remain unbreakable."

With a final squeeze, we let go of each other, knowing that this is just the beginning of a new chapter in our lives. "Remember, Rule One of the oath," I remind us both, and I turn to face the room one more time.

Sarah places a reassuring hand on my shoulder. "Sometimes, Cassie, the answers we seek find their way to us. If it's meant to be unraveled, it will happen. But until then, focus on your journey ahead. Embrace the challenges, embrace the unknown, and let life surprise you."

Her words resonate deep within me, giving me a newfound sense of courage and determination. "You're right, Sarah. I won't let this mystery consume me. I'll focus on building my future, exploring my passions, and making the most of the opportunities that come my way."

We share a knowing smile, both understanding that life is full of mysteries and surprises, but it is up to us to embrace them and forge our own paths.

And so, with a mix of nostalgia and anticipation, I bid farewell to my childhood home and step into the unknown. The journey ahead is uncertain, but I carry with me the love, support, and friendships that have shaped me into the person I have become.

NOT AGAIN!

Almost six years have passed since the fateful mystery with V and the encounters that unfolded. As graduation day from college approaches, I find myself reflecting on the journey I've embarked on, both in pursuit of knowledge and in unraveling the secrets of the past.

Walking through the bustling campus, I feel a familiar hand slip into mine. I turn to see my boyfriend, Alex, by my side. His warm smile and unwavering support have been constant throughout my college years, bringing comfort and stability in the face of challenges.

"Can you believe it, Cassie? Graduation is just around the corner," Alex says, his voice filled with excitement. "We've come so far together, and I couldn't be prouder of you."

I lean into him, a sense of gratitude and contentment washing over me. "I couldn't have done it without you, Alex. Your love and encouragement have been my pillars of strength throughout this journey."

As we pass by the spot where we had our first date, Alex pauses; a grin spreads across his face. "You remember this place, right?" he asks.

I nod, a smile tugging at the corners of my lips. "How could I forget? That's where you stole my heart with your cheesy jokes and genuine charm."

He chuckles, wrapping his arm around my shoulders. "And I've been stealing it ever since. But seriously, Cassie, I'm grateful to have you in my life. You inspire me with your determination, passion, and endless curiosity."

I rest my head against his shoulder, feeling a surge of warmth and love envelop me. "You're my biggest supporter, Alex. Your belief in me has pushed me to reach new heights, and I'm excited to embark on this next chapter of our lives together."

##

Standing on the stage, donning my cap and gown, my heart swells with pride. Graduating with honors, a boyfriend by my side, and a Doctor of Business Administration (DBA) with a Master of Marketing (MM) degree in my hand, I feel a profound sense of accomplishment.

As I scan the crowd, my eyes lock with those of my parents, beaming with pride and joy. They have been my rock, unwavering in their support, and their belief in me has propelled me forward.

A world of opportunities awaits me, with a handful of job offers to choose from. The future is bright, filled with endless possibilities.

At the moment, I think back to the mysterious graduation card and the unanswered questions it holds. Perhaps the true sender will remain unknown forever, and that's okay. Some mysteries are meant to remain unsolved, reminding us that life is full of unexpected twists and turns.

I step off the stage and join my parents, Alex, and my friends Sarah, Tyler, and Sophia, who came to celebrate with me. While basking in the euphoria of my graduation achievement, my phone buzzes in my pocket. I pull it out, my curiosity piqued by the unexpected message. It's a text, and my heart races as I read the words on the screen.

>> *"Congratulations, Cassie, on your remarkable achievement. You've proven yourself to be an extraordinary individual. - V"*

I glance at Sarah, a mix of excitement and intrigue dancing in my eyes. "Sarah, look! It's from V again!"

Her eyebrows shoot up in surprise as she takes a closer look. "No way! The mystery continues! What's it been? Six years of silence? Do you think it's the same person who sent you that card and money?"

I nod, a swirl of emotions churning within me. "It has to be. But who is this V? And why are they reaching out again? There's so much we don't know."

Sarah leans in, her voice filled with anticipation. "You have to reply, Cassie. Maybe this is our chance to uncover the truth. Ask them more, see if they reveal anything."

I take a deep breath, my fingers trembling as I type my response. "Thank you for your kind words. I'm curious to know more about you, about the connection between us. Can you share any further details?"

Time seems to stretch as I wait for a reply, the seconds ticking away with each passing moment. The mystery hangs in the air, the unknown beckoning to be unraveled. And then, the screen illuminates with a new message.

>> *"I'm sorry for the secrecy, Cassie. Some things are best left unsaid. Just know that I've been watching your journey from afar, proud of your accomplishments. Embrace the mystery, for sometimes, the most profound connections are forged through enigma."*

My heart races, a mix of curiosity and trepidation coursing through my veins. "Sarah, I don't know what to make of this," I admit with uncertainty. "Should I keep pursuing this mystery, or should I let it be?"

Sarah places a reassuring hand on my shoulder, her voice filled with wisdom. "Cassie, life is filled with unanswered questions. Sometimes, it's the unanswered that adds depth and beauty to our experiences. Maybe do what they say, embrace the unknown, and let it inspire you rather than consume you."

Her words resonate within me, a reminder that not every mystery needs to be solved and that, sometimes, it's the journey itself that holds the true significance. With a newfound sense of acceptance, I decide to cherish the enigma rather than unraveling it.

89

"But what if there's something important, I'm missing?" I ask, my voice tinged with doubt.

Sarah smiles. "If there's truly something significant, it will find its way to you, Cassie. Sometimes, it's not about seeking answers, but rather allowing them to reveal themselves in due time."

I take a deep breath, feeling a weight lift off my shoulders. "You're right, Sarah. I'll embrace the mystery and trust that if there's more to discover, it will come to light when the time is right."

We exchange a knowing look, a silent acknowledgment of our shared understanding. Sometimes, the unanswered questions in life add an extra layer of depth and excitement. As I turn off my phone, I make a silent promise to myself to continue embracing the unknown, ready to embark on new adventures and create my own story.

The mystery of V will forever be a part of my narrative, a reminder that life's most captivating tales are often woven with unanswered threads. And as I step forward into the vast realm of possibilities, armed with my degree, achievements, and the lessons learned, I am filled with anticipation for the boundless opportunities that lie ahead.

Together, Alex, Sarah, Tyler, Sophia, my parents, and I walk away, leaving the enigmatic messages of V behind me. With a smile on my face and a heart brimming with hope, I step into the next chapter of my life, ready to embrace the mysteries, the wonders, and the endless possibilities that await me.

##

It's been a long day.

Dinner, drinks, and dancing until closing time. Even my parents hit the dance floor. It's adorable seeing them holding hands after all these years.

They're celebrating as much as I am. Their work is done. My future is now wholly in my own hands. Thankfully, the toughest thing I face ahead of me is deciding which of the job offers I will accept.

I climb into my bed, alone. Alex is back in his apartment with Tyler and the gang, so I can have some time with my parents before they leave town tomorrow.

All my focus paid off with four job offers and two more that I'm waiting to hear from. So far, I can go back home, head into Chicago, or even New York. I don't think I'm ready for big city life. Although, I've never been one to shy away from a new adventure.

The crew has spread apart as they graduated. Sarah's back home and owns an art gallery. Sophia is engaged to some guy I've barely met and lives in Chicago, and Tyler is a social media influencer who travels the globe with a buddy of his, documenting great places to travel on a dime.

I'm the last of the crew to graduate college, and it's time to get serious about my future. I feel like everyone found their passion and purpose, and I found degrees and jobs.

I don't know when Alex will propose, but he's put up with me for almost four years, so I have to assume that's coming soon.

I think I love him. Even if we don't get married right away, we definitely need to figure out what our future looks like.

Cassandra Vida Montgomery. I try the name on for size, wondering how I've never even strung the names together until this very moment.

Cassie Montgomery. That doesn't sound so bad, but does it sound like me?

Jesus, woman, can you ever stop thinking and trying to control everything? I accuse myself, knowing the answer. It's just the way I'm wired. I honestly don't know how Alex tolerates me. He's been this gentle giant since the day we met that first week of college. We've grown up together.

Even when he graduated last year, he decided to stay here and wait for me. That's dedication. I wonder if he's been waiting for graduation to propose. If so, I guess I have something to look forward to very soon now.

I roll over and fluff my pillow. It feels weird lying here without him. It's not like my parents don't know we're sleeping together. I called home to tell my mom the very next day. It's all about logistics tonight, but the bed sure does feel empty.

I grab my phone and find his name.

<< *Night, babe.*

...

>> *Good night, sweetheart. I'll see you in the morning. I'm going back to sleep now.*

93

Of course, he's sleeping like a baby and probably doesn't even miss me. I scroll through emails and rapid-delete to clear my inbox. I'm too OCD to let emails linger. Next, onto the texts. Oh, damn. I almost forgot it was just earlier today that V texted me again. I reread our conversation.

My mind swirls with thoughts, ideas, and plots on how to trap them into telling me who they are.

No. I couldn't.

But, I wonder if it'd work?

Sarah will flip out.

I pull up the conversation with "V" again. Reading a dozen more times.

I type...

<< I know who you are. I know everything! You didn't need to keep it a secret.

... and I wait.

All In or Nothing

Drama/Romance

https://www.amazon.com/dp/B0B7FW9W8M

Forbidden Love (18+)

Steamy Romance/Drama

https://www.amazon.com/dp/B0B5SX24SX

Sydney Brown Presents

Varied/Compilation

https://www.amazon.com/dp/B0BSBT36HN

Legends Reborn

Sci-Fi/Fantasy

https://www.amazon.com/dp/B0B5QB79KL

From A to Z: A Year of Essential Terms and Concepts

Dictionary/Education

https://www.amazon.com/dp/B0B62XJY59

The Great Ascension

Education/Business

https://www.amazon.com/dp/B09Y89V7XL

Sydney Brown, a multi-best-selling author, and visionary publisher, goes beyond her own literary achievements by collaborating with individuals to bring their stories to life. With a passion for empowering aspiring writers, Sydney locks arms with them, guiding and supporting them through the publishing phase.

Sydney ensures that talented authors receive the guidance and resources they need to navigate the complex world of publishing. Sydney's collaborative approach allows aspiring writers to realize their dreams of becoming published authors.

In addition to her publishing endeavors, Sydney is committed to sharing her knowledge and expertise with aspiring writers through the "I'm the Writer" program. This comprehensive program equips participants with the tools and skills needed to craft compelling fiction and pursue a successful career as a certified freelance writer.

Connect with Sydney on social media at @JustSydneyBrown. Discover the invaluable resources and support she offers aspiring authors and unlock the potential within you to become a skilled storyteller. Together, through collaboration and education, Sydney Brown paves the way for aspiring writers to achieve their literary aspirations and make their mark in the world.

CONTACT US!

Want to learn how to write your own memoir or get some bite-sized writing advice? Find the YouTube channel here.

https://www.youtube.com/@justsydneybrown

You can find the TLM Publishing House Facebook page here. Go here if you want to join our Advanced Reader Copy (ARC) list for upcoming titles!

https://www.facebook.com/tlmpublishinghouse

While you're there, why not join the Aspiring Writers Facebook group as well?

https://www.facebook.com/groups/aspiring

www.ingramcontent.com/pod-product-compliance
Lightning Source LLC
Chambersburg PA
CBHW070636130626
46555CB00006B/2572